FOR *Mike Carty*, A TRUE CHAMPION OF OTHERS

Text and illustrations © 2018 Kelly Collier

All rights reserved. No part of this publication may be reproduced, stored in a retrieval system or transmitted, in any form or by any means, without the prior written permission of Kids Can Press Ltd. or, in case of photocopying or other reprographic copying, a license from The Canadian Copyright Licensing Agency (Access Copyright). For an Access Copyright license, visit www.accesscopyright.ca or call toll free to 1-800-893-5777.

Kids Can Press gratefully acknowledges the financial support of the Government of Ontario, through the Ontario Media Development Corporation; the Ontario Arts Council; the Canada Council for the Arts; and the Government of Canada, through the CBF, for our publishing activity.

Published in Canada and the U.S. by Kids Can Press Ltd.
25 Dockside Drive, Toronto, ON M5A 0B5

www.kidscanpress.com

Kids Can Press is a Corus Entertainment Inc. company

The artwork in this book was rendered in ink and watercolor, and finished in Photoshop.
The text is set in Lemon Yellow Sun and Mulberry Script Pro.

Edited by Yasemin Uçar
Designed by Karen Powers and Julia Naimska

Printed and bound in Shenzhen, China, in 3/2018, through C & C Offset
CM 18 0 9 8 7 6 5 4 3 2 1

LIBRARY AND ARCHIVES CANADA CATALOGUING IN PUBLICATION

Collier, Kelly (Kelly M.), author, illustrator
Team Steve / written and illustrated by Kelly Collier.

(Steve the horse)
ISBN 978-1-77138-932-7 (hardcover)

I. Title.

PS8605.O458T43 2018   jC813'.6   C2017-907198-X

* STEVE THE HORSE *

TEAM Steve

WRITTEN AND
ILLUSTRATED BY KELLY COLLIER

KIDS CAN PRESS

SPRING IS HERE!
Steve LOVES SPRING BECAUSE
THAT MEANS IT'S TIME FOR THE
ANNUAL RACE-A-THON!

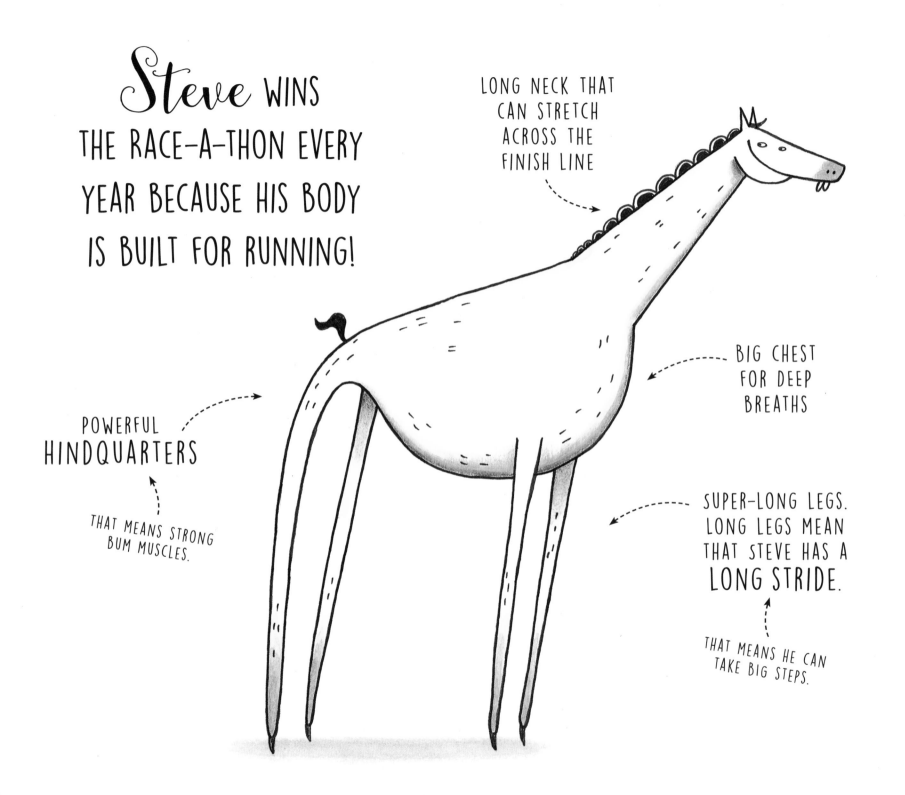

BOB EXPLAINS THAT A RELAY
IS A RACE BETWEEN **TEAMS**.
A TEAM HAS FOUR RUNNERS,
WHO EACH HAVE TO RUN
A SECTION OF THE RACE.

"NO PROBLEMO!" SAYS Steve.
"I WILL BE ON A TEAM WITH DEER, RABBIT
AND ... HMM, WHO ELSE IS FAST?
... OH, AND FOX!"

"UMM ..." SAYS BOB. "THE THING IS, TO KEEP THE RACE FAIR, WE DREW NAMES. YOU'RE ON A TEAM WITH DUCK, TURTLE AND SNAIL."

UH-HUH ...

"WAIT A SEC ..." SAYS Steve. "A DUCK **WADDLES**, A TURTLE **WALKS** AND A SNAIL ... IS A **SNAIL!** HOW ARE WE SUPPOSED TO WIN?"

"I DON'T KNOW, STEVE, BUT GOOD LUCK FIGURING THAT OUT," SAYS BOB.

Steve DECIDES
HE'S GOING TO BE THE
BEST. COACH. EVER.

AFTER ALL, WINNING A RACE HAS PROBABLY BEEN
A LIFELONG DREAM FOR HIS TEAMMATES.

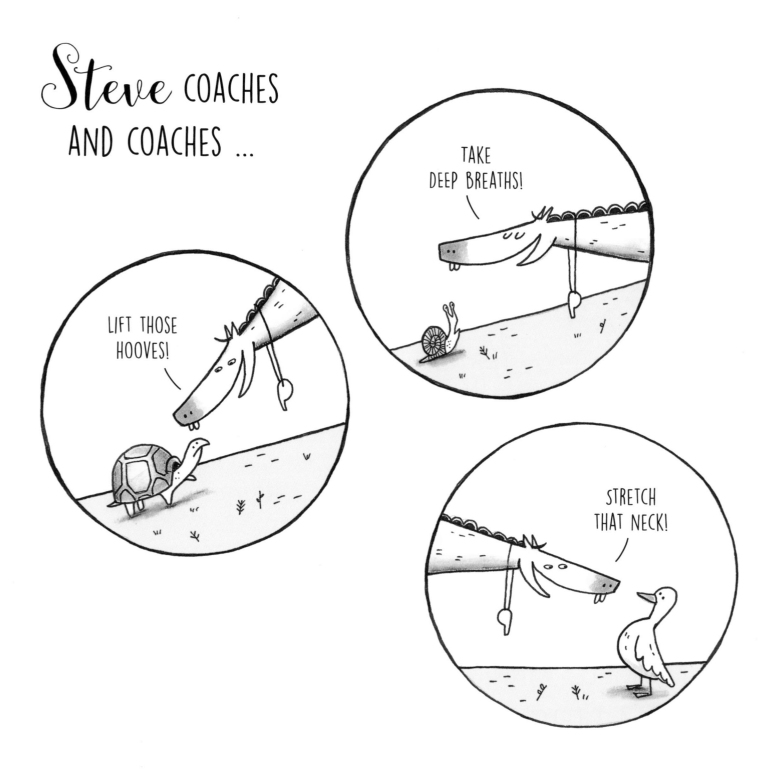

AND GIVES LOTS AND LOTS OF ADVICE (MAYBE MORE THAN NECESSARY) ...

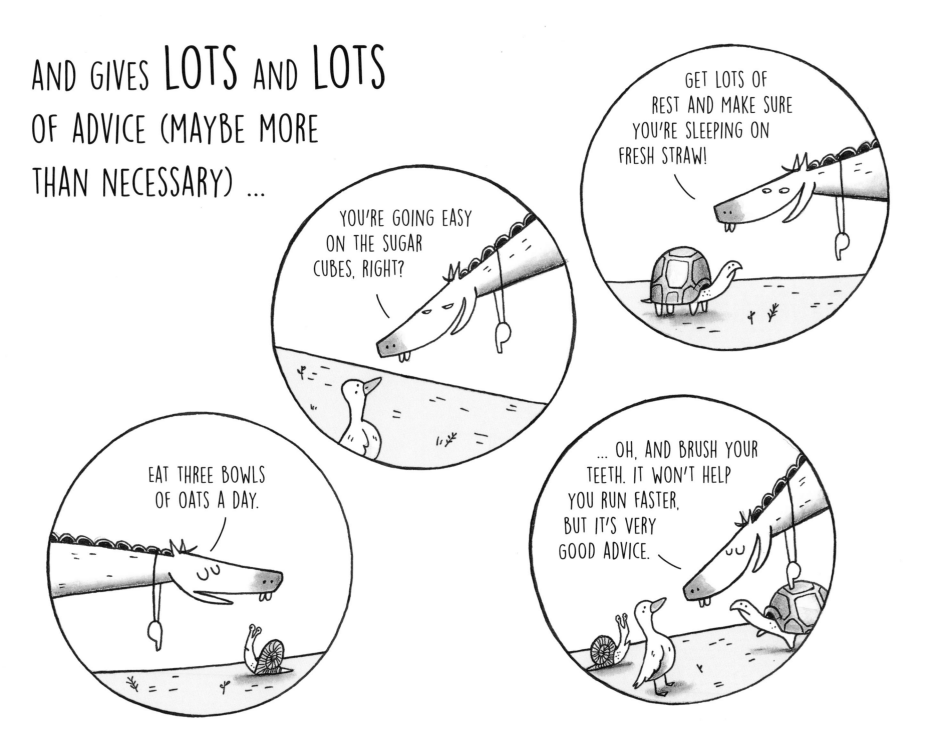

THE RACERS FIND THEIR POSTS ...

AND THE RACE BEGINS.

TURTLE IS SLOW OFF THE MARK.
BUT DEER IS OFF LIKE A SHOT,
AND SKUNK IS HOT ON HIS HEELS.

MEANWHILE, AT POST FOUR, Steve IS ROOTING FOR HIS TEAM.

GO, TURTLE!

Steve PICKS UP HIS HOOVES.
HE TAKES **DEEP** BREATHS.

HE STRETCHES HIS NECK LONG TO REACH THE FINISH LINE. AND ...

THE OTHER TWO TEAMS HAVE
TIED FOR FIRST PLACE!

Steve FEELS AWFUL. (AND A LITTLE EMBARRASSED.)

"THANKS TO YOUR COACHING, WE WERE ALL FASTER THAN WE EVER WERE BEFORE," SAYS DUCK.

"THAT'S TRUE ..." SAYS Steve.
"AND ALSO, BY LOSING, I HELPED TWO TEAMS TO WIN!"

AND THAT MEANS I'M AN EVEN BETTER COACH THAN I THOUGHT!

I GUESS SO!

SURE, STEVE.

IF IT MAKES YOU FEEL BETTER, THEN YEAH.